Deep Breaths

In memory of Brian Anson: friend, artist, and storyteller

Copyright © 2010 by Carol Thompson

All rights reserved. Published in the United States by Rodale Kids,
an imprint of Random House Children's Books, a division of Penguin Random House LLC, New York.
Originally published in Australia as *Chill* in 2010 and subsequently published as *Dolly & Jack: Deep Breaths*
in 2018 by Little Hare Books, an imprint of Hardie Grant Egmont, Richmond, Victoria.
First published in the United States as *I Like You Best* by Holiday House, New York, in 2011.

Rodale and the colophon are registered trademarks and
Rodale Kids is a trademark of Penguin Random House LLC.

Visit us on the Web! rhcbooks.com

Educators and librarians, for a variety of teaching tools,
visit us at RHTeachersLibrarians.com

Library of Congress Cataloging-in-Publication Data is available upon request.
ISBN 978-1-9848-9397-0 (trade) — ISBN 978-1-9848-9398-7 (ebook)

MANUFACTURED IN CHINA
10 9 8 7 6 5 4 3 2 1
2019 Rodale Kids Edition

Deep Breaths

Carol Thompson

RODALE KiDS

Dolly likes to play on her own.

Dum-di-dum-di-dum!

Especially the mirror game.

But some games are not much fun all alone.

Then . . .

along comes Jack the Rabbit,

Dolly's best friend in all the world.

Some days Jack and Dolly
are quiet together.
They go to their Best Place
and watch the clouds . . .

...or listen to their favorite music.

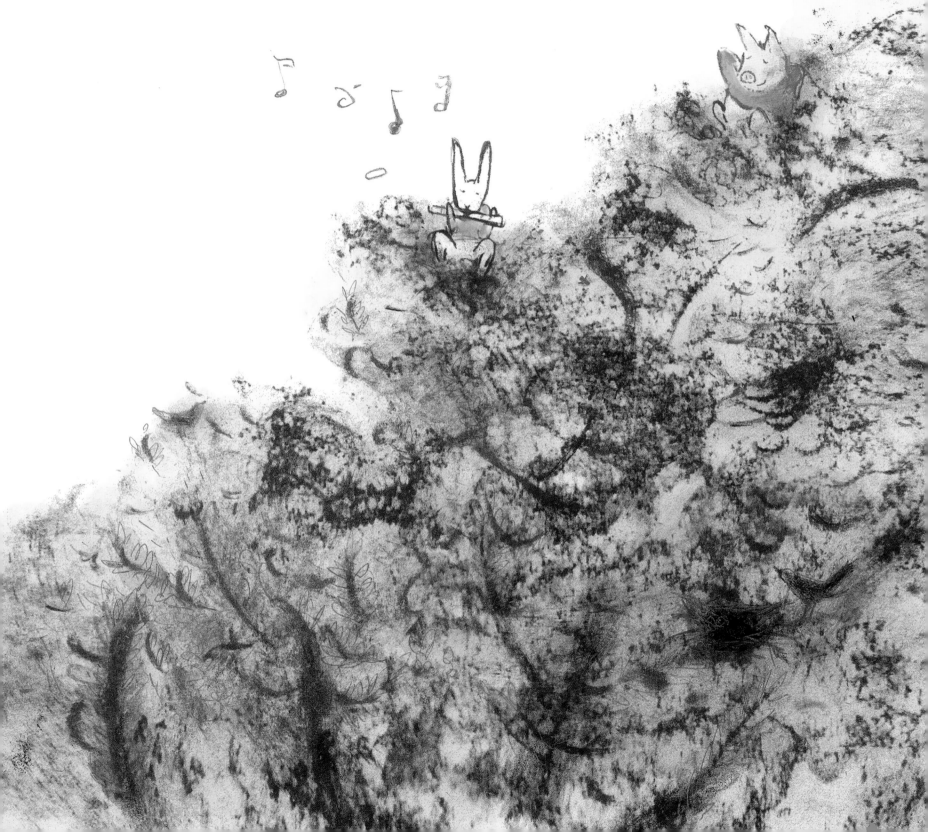

Some days they race around so fast

and play so hard,

all they can do is . . .

One day, when Dolly goes to visit Jack,
he's wearing a beret.

Jack paints a big circle.
And then some smaller circles.
Dolly paints some long wobbly lines.

Dolly looks at Jack's picture.

Jack looks at Dolly's picture.

Dolly takes a deep breath.
All the way in and all the way out.

Dolly takes a
lovely warm bath.
She closes her
eyes and thinks
of something she
likes a lot.

Jack counts slowly up to ten,
and back down again.
And up again!

He closes his
eyes and thinks
of something he
likes a lot.

The next day . . .

Dolly goes to her Best Place.

Jack goes to his Best Place.